For Maureen and John

First published 2011 by Macmillan Children's Books a division of Macmillan Publishers Limited

20 New Wharf Road, London N1 9RR

Basingstoke and Oxford Associated companies throughout the world

ISBN: 978-0-230-70425-1

Copyright © Emily Gravett 2011 Moral rights asserted. All rights reserved.

10 9 8 7 6 5 4 3 2 1

A CIP catalogue record for this book is available from the British Library

www.panmacmillan.com

www.emilygravett.com

Printed in Belgium by Proost

I can dress him in a bow...

I can make him jump

through hoops!

I can lift him off the ground!

I can make him dance a jig but...

through the air!

We can even
place our heads

between his

mighty
jaws

but WOLF WON'T...